This book belongs to:

....

....

For Isabelle, Flynn, Phoebe, and Ruby - A. H. Benjamin

For Ben and Amy - Bill Bolton

A NEW BURLINGTON BOOK
The Old Brewery
6 Blundell Street
London N7 9BH

Editor: Alexandra Koken
Designer: Verity Clark

Copyright © QEB Publishing 2013

First published in the United States by
QEB Publishing, Inc., 3 Wrigley, Suite A, Irvine, CA 92618

www.qed-publishing.co.uk

A CIP record for this book is available from the Library of Congress.

ISBN 978 1 78171 379 2

Printed in China

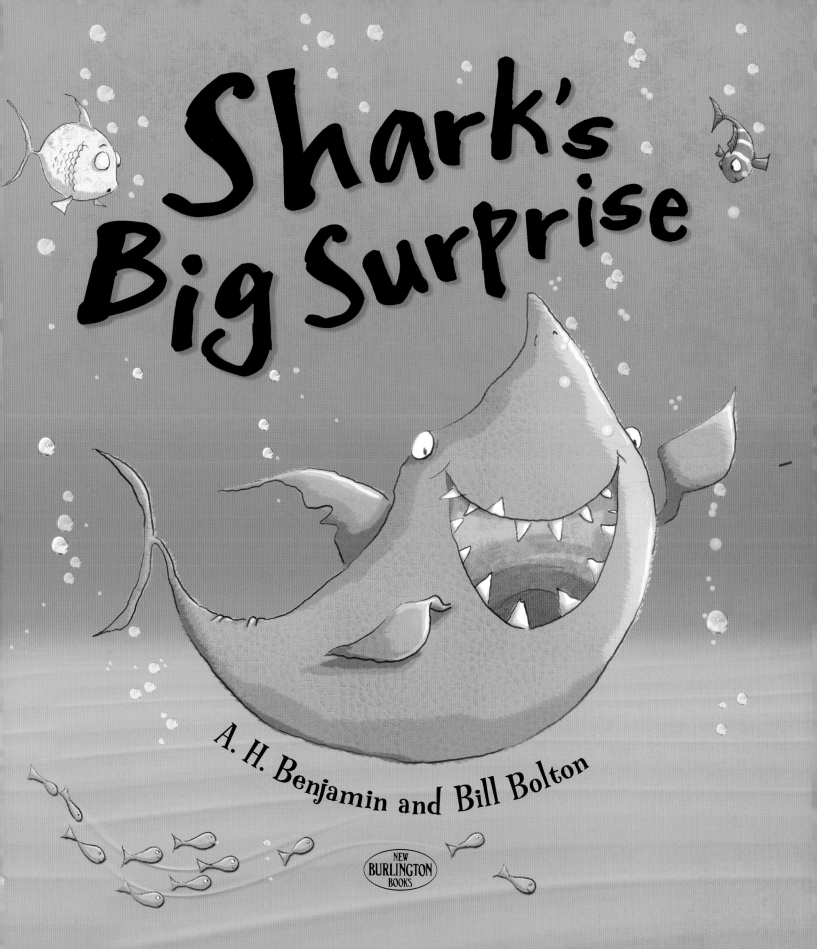

Shark's Big Surprise

A. H. Benjamin and Bill Bolton

NEW
BURLINGTON
BOOKS

Shark had sharp, pointy teeth.
He looked scary. Everyone hid from him.

"It's not *fair*,"
he thought sadly.

"No one wants
to play
with me."

One day, Shark had an idea. The idea kept
him busy all day. When he was ready, he left
the old, sunken ship where he lived. . .

Shark lurked behind a large rock.
Soon Octopus came along, his
long arms
splish-
splashing.

Shark hid inside the thick seaweed.

Soon Lobster appeared, her sharp pincers click-clacking.

Shark slid into a dark
cave, and waited.

Before long Turtle
paddled by, his large
flippers flip-
flapping.

Shark pounced.

Next, Shark hid behind a sandy mound.
Jellyfish wobbled by, her thin

tentacles swish-swoshing.

Shark **POUNCED.** **"Got you!"** he snapped. And he put Jellyfish in the bag.

"Let me out!" said Jellyfish.

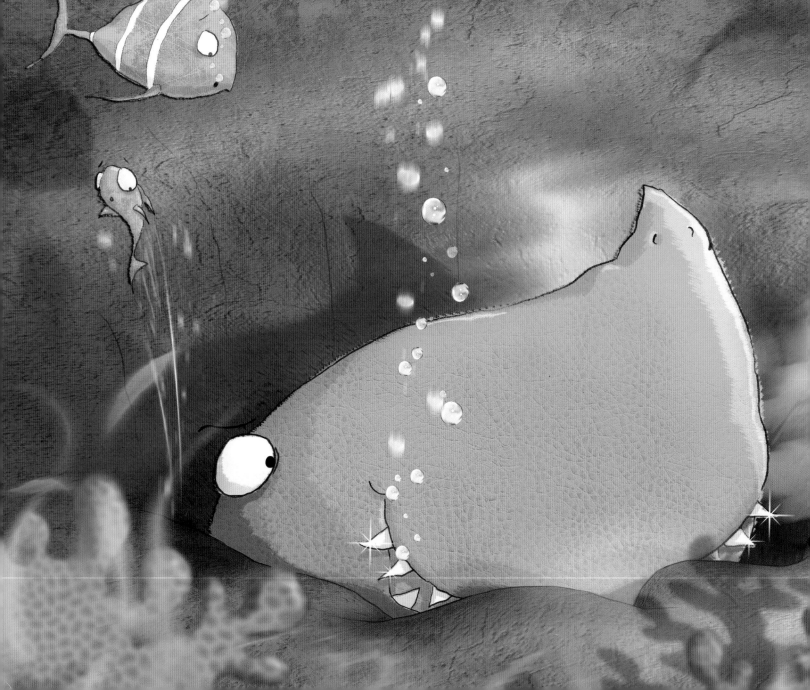

Shark had not finished yet! He slipped into a deep hole.
Soon Starfish crawled along, her spiky arms

plip-plopping.

Shark **pounced** once more.

Soon Starfish was
in Shark's bag.

"I think I have enough," said
Shark, holding his bag full of fish.
"Oh, I'm
so hungry!"
he said, setting off for home.

Soon Shark was back at home.

"I'm so pleased," he said

as he emptied his bag.

Everyone was terrified as they tumbled out.

"It's the end of us!"

Lobster wailed.

Suddenly Shark turned around and said...

"You gave us quite a scare," said Octopus. "Next time you want us to join you for cake, you could just ask…"

Next steps

Sharks can be dangerous animals that look scary. What do the children think of the shark in our story? Do they think he's scary too? Explain that the other creatures in the book are only afraid of him because he looks fierce—but Shark can't help what he looks like. He just wants to make friends.

Talk about facial expressions. Ask the children to draw faces with different emotions: happy, sad, angry, surprised, and so on. How do they think the creatures feel in the book?

See if the children can recognize some of the sea creatures in the story. Have they seen any of them in real life? Can they give the characters proper names? Like Terry the Turtle, or Lucy the Lobster?

Discuss other sea creatures. Do the children have a favorite one? Would they like one as a pet? How about a shark?

Ask the children what kind of surprise they would like. What is the best surprise they've had? Can they describe how they felt? Sometimes it's nice to surprise someone you like. Ask the children how they would surprise a friend.

Try and find some facts about sharks. There are about 350 species. They come in different sizes. The smallest is no longer than 6 inches (15 centimeters). The biggest can be over 39 feet (12 meters) long!